The Merchant of Venice

Written by William Shakespeare

Retold by Jon Mayhew

Illustrated by Mona Meslier Menuau

Cast of characters

Portia/Balthasar

Bassanio

Antonio

Shylock

Prince of Morocco

Nerissa

the judge

Prince of Aragon

1 Too many princes

Portia was the luckiest girl in the world. She was the saddest too. She sat at the long dinner table, which was covered in plates of rich food, roast chicken, duck, venison and beef, and sighed. There were steaming bowls of vegetables glazed in butter. But she wasn't hungry. Her own minstrels played sweet music to the guests at the feast. But she wasn't listening.

She should've been happy. She had so much money, she'd lost count of it, and she was famous too. She lived in a beautiful palace in a place called Belmont. Every handsome, wealthy young man at that feast had arrived just to see if he could win Portia's hand in marriage.

"And that's the problem, really," she huffed to herself. "All these silly men from the four corners of the world showing off and trying to impress me!"

A prince dressed in the finest silk shirt bowed to Portia. "My lady, your golden hair dazzles me, as do your bewitching emerald eyes," he said, grasping her hand. "They remind me of my horse, Cloppy. Apart from you, he's the love of my life. Strong and swift. He can jump a hay cart without blinking …"

Portia pulled her hand away. "Cloppy?" she gasped. "You just compared me to a horse!"

"Horses are great," the prince said, grinning. "They're my favourite thing!"

Portia felt her anger rising. "Why, of all the …"

Another young man interrupted. *"Monsieur!"* he snapped at the prince. "You've offended Madame Portia and now I, Monsieur Le Bon, will challenge you to a duel to defend her honour!"

"No!" Portia said, feeling her head begin to ache. "You really don't have to."

But Monsieur Le Bon drew his sword. *"En garde!"* he shouted.

The prince raised his hands and staggered backwards, knocking over a chair and spilling another young man's soup.

"Oof!" said the man.

The soup splashed on to a snoozing duke's knee.

"Aaaargh!" screamed the duke. He head-butted a servant carrying a jug of custard.

"Oow!" cried the servant, who tipped custard all over a nobleman's head.

"Glub," said the nobleman, his mouth full of custard. "Mmm. Custard!"

Soon, tables were tipped over, chairs were flying and all the men were arguing with each other.

Someone grabbed Portia's hand. She looked down to see Nerissa, her maid.

"My lady," Nerissa said. "Maybe you should come into the garden!" She lowered her voice and whispered, "Before someone gets really hurt!"

Portia couldn't help grinning. Nerissa was more than just a servant; she was Portia's best friend.

The garden felt cool compared to the busy feasting hall stuffed with arrogant men strutting about. It was much quieter too!

Portia plonked herself down on a bench. "What am I going to do, Nerissa? Ever since my father died, I've had a constant stream of men trying to get me to marry them. They're only interested in my money and my land!"

"But that's why your father made up the test!" Nerissa said, patting her hand. "You'll see, once half of these gentlemen realise what they have to risk in order to marry you, they'll go home."

"I wish they'd *all* go home," Portia groaned. "I don't want to marry any of them. Even if they've passed father's test."

"I know someone you'd marry if he came along," Nerissa grinned, giving Portia a nudge. "Do you remember that young man called Bassanio who visited before your father passed away?"

Portia felt herself blushing. "He *was* nice," she admitted, "but he kept losing all his money." She gave another sigh. "Anyway, even if he did come here, he'd have to take the test like everyone else. I couldn't *choose* to marry him."

Before Nerissa could answer, the sound of trumpets split the air and Portia saw a handsome man dressed in flowing robes striding across the perfect lawns of the garden.

"It's the Prince of Morocco," Nerissa gasped. "The first man to take the test. He might win the chance to be your husband!"

"Oh no," Portia moaned.

The Prince of Morocco bowed low to Portia and kissed her hand. "It's a great honour, my lady, and I've travelled many miles to try to win your love."

"O-oh!" Portia stammered. "Y-yes, lovely to meet you too."

The Prince of Morocco raised his chin. "Enough of this small talk. I'm a man of action!" he said. "Let me go and try to win!"

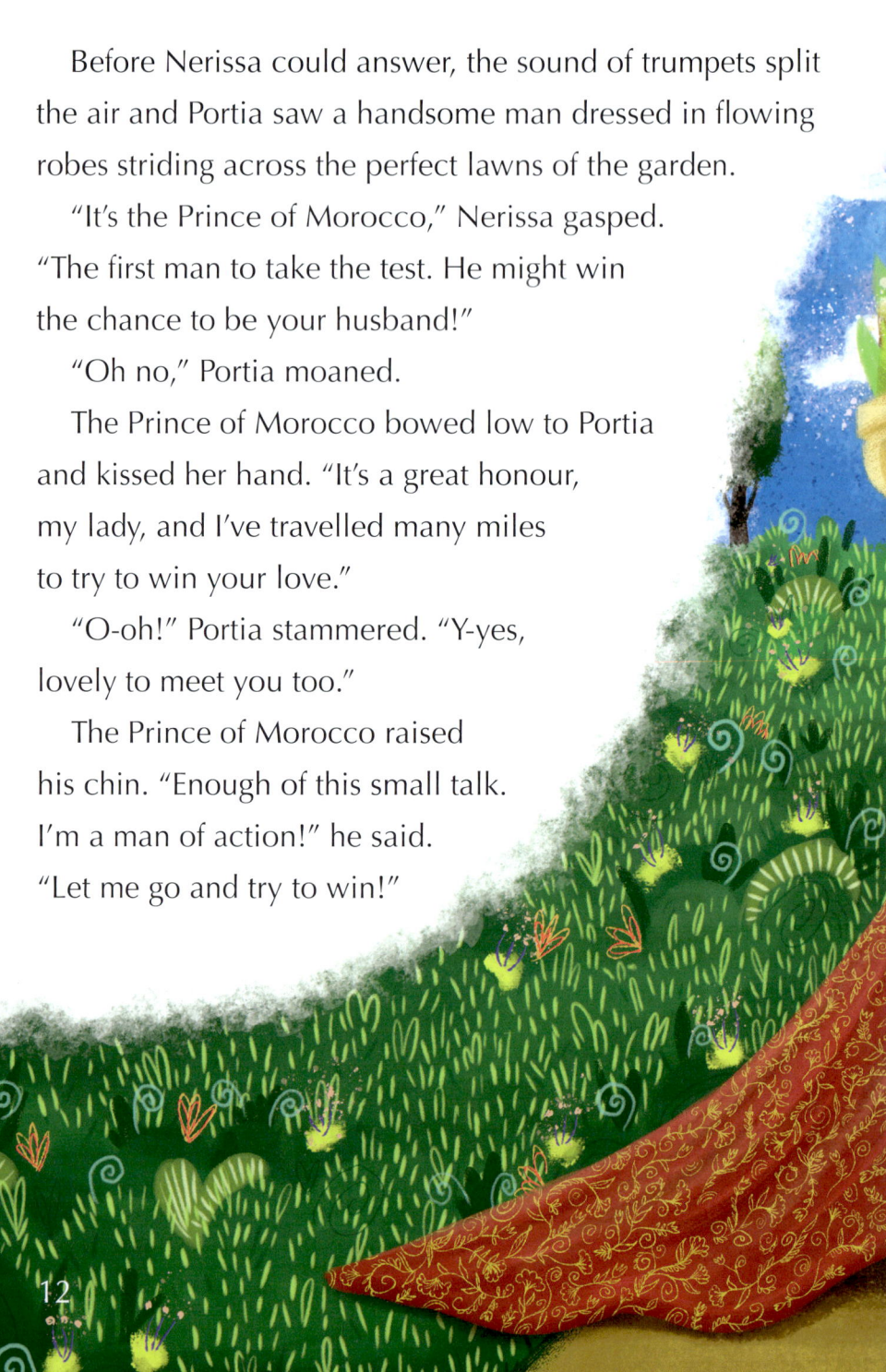

2 The test

Nerissa and Portia led the Prince of Morocco into a large hall. At one end of the hall stood a table with three small chests – one made of gold, one made of silver and one made of dull, grey lead. A notice stood next to each chest.

"Now, my prince," Nerissa said, stepping forward. "According to the rules of the test left by Lady Portia's father, you must choose one of the chests on the table. If it has a portrait of her in it, then she'll marry you. If it doesn't then you must leave and never marry anyone else again ever. It's a solemn promise that you mustn't break."

The Prince of Morocco looked from Portia to Nerissa and bowed. "I agree to the rules. If I can't marry Portia, then I never want to marry anyone!"

"Are you sure?" Portia said, feeling sorry for the prince. "You'll have to live alone for the rest of your life!"

"It's a risk worth taking. For your beautiful face, I'd fight lions with my bare hands," the Prince of Morocco said. He turned to the chests. "Now let me read these signs and think."

He looked at the gold chest and read the sign. "'Who chooses me shall gain what many men desire'," he read. "The silver chest's sign says, 'Who chooses me shall get as much as he deserves'. The last chest says, 'Who chooses me must give and risk all he has'."

Portia bit her lip as the Prince of Morocco's bejewelled hand hovered over each box. He looked over to her but she glanced away; she'd promised her father on his deathbed that she wouldn't help the contestants in any way.

"Hmmm," the prince said, stroking his black beard. "It can't be the lead box; I won't be giving anything if I marry Portia and it wouldn't be a risk for me." His hand moved to the silver box. "The silver box gives as much as I deserve. I do deserve to marry her, it's true – "

"He thinks a lot of himself," Portia whispered to Nerissa.

The Prince of Morocco shook his head. "But the gold chest gives what many men desire. Aren't there many men here? All desiring to marry the beautiful Portia? It must be this one!" He picked up the key to the gold chest and unlocked it.

Portia held her breath as the prince looked inside. Then he pulled a scroll of paper from the chest. "Oh no!" he cried. "No picture! No Portia. I've just got a rhyme."

He held up the paper and Portia read:

"All that glitters is not gold;

Fare you well; your love is cold."

The Prince of Morocco threw down the paper and stormed from the hall. Portia couldn't help feeling sorry for him.

"Don't worry," Nerissa said. "He loved himself more than you."

A servant appeared at the door of the hall. "My lady," he said, "a young Venetian merchant has arrived to take the test."

Nerissa ran over to the window and looked out. "It's Bassanio!" she cried. "Your long-lost Bassanio!"

"Oh no!" Portia groaned, slumping her shoulders.

"But this is good news," Nerissa said. "He might win!"

"He might not get the chance," Portia complained. "It's the Prince of Aragon's turn next. What if he wins first?"

3 The arrogant Prince of Aragon

Portia disliked the Prince of Aragon the moment she set eyes on him. He was standing with his pointed beard held in the air and looked down his long nose at her.

"I've come to win your hand in marriage!" he announced. "You lucky girl!"

What a big head! Portia thought but she nodded politely and pointed to the boxes. "You know the rules, my prince. Make your choice."

The Prince of Aragon nodded. "I agree!" He stared at each box in turn. "Pah! Gold. Every commoner would choose that. But I'm a prince!" He looked at the lead box. "Pah! Lead. A horrible, dull metal. Not at all suitable for one as noble and handsome as me!" He turned to Portia and gave her a crooked grin.

"Oh, hurry up!" she muttered under her breath. Her heart was pounding. Somewhere in the building, Bassanio waited for her, and this stupid prince might spoil everything.

"What have we here?" the prince said, picking up the silver box. He read the sign: "'Who chooses me shall get as much as he deserves'. Why, am I not the Prince of Aragon? Do I not deserve the best? I'll open this one, give me the key!" He clicked his fingers at Nerissa impatiently, as she handed him the key to the box.

The prince's face fell and his cheeks grew red. "What's this?" he hissed, holding up a toy clown's head. "Do you take me for a fool?"

Nerissa picked up the sheet of paper that the prince had dropped in his rage and read it to him:

"Some of the biggest fools, it's true,

Are covered with silver and so are you!"

Pale with fury, the Prince of Aragon slammed the box down and stormed out of the hall without even saying goodbye.

Portia heaved a sigh of relief. "Thank goodness for that!" she said to Nerissa. "He was so rude and arrogant, I don't think I could've married him!"

But Nerissa had a sly grin on her face and had hurried over to the doors. "My lady, it's Bassanio!" she said, flinging them open.

Bassanio gave a deep bow. He looked just as Portia remembered him from all those years ago: tall and strong, with dark hair and glittering brown eyes. He was dressed a lot better than when she last saw him. Once he'd worn a travel-stained leather coat; now his velvet jacket looked as dark as midnight with not a mark on it. Jewels covered his fingers and a feathered hat crowned his head.

"It's wonderful to see you again," Portia said. "I've never forgotten you, Bassanio. But I see you've done well for yourself. Last time we met, you were a poor soldier."

"I'm overjoyed to see you too," Bassanio said. "I've come to try my luck and choose one of these boxes."

"I hope you win," Portia said, clasping his hands in hers. "But what if you choose the wrong box?"

Bassanio frowned. "I don't care. I can't wait. I must know if we can marry straight away!"

He strode over to the boxes, while Portia watched, biting her lip. "Hmmm," Bassanio said, lifting the golden box. "Too obvious. Every man might want gold but look what happened to King Midas! I want something better than gold. I want love!"

He looked closely at the silver box. "The silver box looks pretty on the outside, but it's what's inside that counts."

Finally, he turned to the lead box. "This box is dull and plain. It isn't showy like the others." He read out the sign: "'Who chooses me must give and risk all he has'. I'd give everything I have to Portia and risk everything for her. So I choose this ordinary looking lead box!"

Nerissa gave him the key and he opened the box, pulling out a portrait of Portia.

"You did it!" Portia said, rushing over to hug Bassanio. "Now we can be married!"

Bassanio grinned, but then he pulled away. He looked sad. "Portia, I haven't told you everything," he said. "I must tell you the truth and then you might not want to marry me!"

4 Good news, bad news

Portia looked at Bassanio's troubled face and began to wonder what it was he was about to tell her. Was he a murderer perhaps? Or a pirate?

"You see, Portia," Bassanio sighed, "the truth is I'm not really rich. In fact, I've no money at all! I borrowed it from a good friend of mine, a merchant called Antonio."

Portia's heart lifted. "Oh, thank goodness for that!"

"You mean, you don't mind?" Bassanio said, looking at her with wide eyes. "I thought you wouldn't look at me unless I had the best clothes and the finest jewels."

Portia sighed. "Haven't you learnt anything from the test of the boxes?" she said. "It's what's on the inside that counts, not how rich you are or how well-dressed or handsome you think you look!"

Bassanio hugged her. "Then let's prepare a feast and a wedding!" he said.

28

29

The preparations for the wedding began. Servants hurried to cook fine food and arrange flowers all around Portia's palace. Musicians played in the great hall and everyone was happy – but not for long. That night, a violent storm blew in from the sea, blowing out candles and making the people of Venice close their shutters and light the fires to keep warm.

The next morning, Portia was in her room, trying to decide which dress to wear for her wedding, when there was a knock on her door. It was Bassanio.

"My love, why do you look so sad?" Portia asked. "Have you had some bad news?"

"Very bad," Bassanio sighed. "It's my friend Antonio. He's in trouble."

"What kind of trouble?"

Bassanio gave another deep sigh. "I told you I borrowed some money from Antonio."

"Yes," Portia said. "And it doesn't matter."

"The trouble is, Antonio didn't have the money either," Bassanio explained. "Or he did, but he'd used it to buy ships that were carrying rich silks from China, spices from India and gold from Mexico. Once his ships had reached Venice and the cargo was unloaded, he'd be a very rich man indeed."

Portia shook her head in disbelief. "So he borrowed the money from someone else to lend to you?" she said.

Bassanio nodded. "The terrible storm last night sank all of Antonio's ships. He has nothing and can't repay the money he borrowed for me!"

"How much did he borrow?" Portia asked.

"3,000 gold ducats," Bassanio replied.

Portia shrugged. "No problem," she said. "I've more than enough money, and once we're married, we can repay your friend's debt three times over."

But Bassanio still didn't look happy. "You don't understand," he said. "Antonio borrowed the money from a merchant called Shylock. Antonio and Shylock hate each other, they always have. But Shylock was the only man who'd lend Antonio the money. He made a deal with Antonio that he'd lend him the money, but that if he couldn't pay it back, Shylock would be able to claim repayment by cutting a pound of flesh from any part of Antonio's body."

Portia shivered. "That's horrible, a pound weighs a lot – it's like his whole heart," she gasped. "It'll kill him."

"I know," Bassanio said. "I tried and tried to persuade Antonio not to agree to the deal, but he wouldn't listen. And I guess Shylock saw it as a way to get Antonio in his power. As I said, they hate each other. Both are successful merchants in Venice; they're always trying to outsmart each other."

"So, now Antonio's ships have sunk and he has no money, Shylock's going to claim his pound of flesh," Portia said. "Why must some men be so arrogant and competitive all the time?"

"Antonio's in prison. He'll be taken to court and the judge will decide if Shylock can claim what my friend owes him," Bassanio said. "I must go and help Antonio!"

Portia grabbed his hand. "We'll get married first," she said. "Then you can offer Shylock as much gold as he wants to save Antonio."

The wedding was quick and, even though they were worried about Antonio, both Portia and Bassanio felt so happy.

"Here," Portia said, sliding a ring on to Bassanio's finger. "Take this ring and promise me that you'll keep it safe."

Bassanio kissed her. "I'll die before I part with this ring," he said. He held up a heavy bag. "And with the gold ducats you gave me, I'll return with my friend Antonio!"

Portia watched him as he made his way to his boat, and then she hurried to her room calling for Nerissa.

"What are you up to?" Nerissa said, as she watched Portia packing clothes into a bag.

Portia tapped her nose. "You don't think I'd trust Bassanio to rescue his best friend alone, do you?" she said. "I have a plan!"

5 The trial

People squeezed into the courtroom to see what the judge had to say about Antonio and Shylock. Bassanio felt so hot that he thought he'd pass out. He could hardly breathe and the big bag of gold ducats he'd brought with him to pay Shylock felt very heavy.

The judge smacked his hammer down and brought the crowd to silence. "Antonio. Shylock says he lent you 3,000 gold ducats and you agreed that if you couldn't pay him back, he could cut a pound of flesh from anywhere on your body. Is that true?"

Bassanio could see Antonio's grey-haired head sink as he nodded. "It's true, your honour."

The judge looked at Shylock.

"That's true," Shylock said. "If he couldn't pay, he shouldn't have borrowed the money."

"But don't you realise that if you cut a pound of flesh from Antonio, he's probably going to die?" the judge said.

Shylock shrugged. "He might not. Anyway, that was the deal."

"I'll pay the debt!" Bassanio shouted, pushing through the crowd and lifting his bag of gold ducats. "Here! I've three times what you're owed if you let Antonio go!"

The room exploded into noise and the judge had to bang his hammer down again.

"This is Bassanio, your honour," Antonio said. "A dear friend."

The judge turned to Shylock. "Well, Shylock," he said, "it seems you have your payment."

But Shylock shook his head. "That wasn't what we agreed. Bassanio doesn't owe me the money, Antonio does, and I'm going to teach him a lesson! I want my pound of flesh!"

The crowd gasped.

Before the judge could reply, a servant hurried forward and whispered in his ear. "It seems," the judge said, "that we've a wise lawyer here to defend Antonio. Let him in. Maybe he can make Shylock see reason."

A young man in a dark cloak and hat swept into the courtroom. "I'm Balthasar, a learned lawyer," he said. "Where's the merchant called Shylock?"

"I'm here," Shylock said, raising his hand.

"And so you must be Antonio," Balthasar said to Antonio. He turned to Shylock. "Sir, have you not just been offered three times the amount of money you were owed? Why won't you take it?"

Shylock narrowed his eyes. "Ask Antonio what *he'd* do if *I* owed him the money!"

Balthasar looked at Antonio who went very red. "I wouldn't take the money, either," he muttered. "We're men of business. Merchants. We live … and die by our promises."

"You're a pair of fools," Balthasar muttered. He turned to Shylock. "Give me the contract that you both signed to make this agreement legal."

Shylock handed the paper over and Balthasar read it, humming and nodding. "Ah," he said, nodding. "I see. Yes. Pound of flesh. Very well." He rolled the paper up and looked around the court. "It seems that the contract's correct. Antonio owes Shylock a pound of flesh and Shylock has every right to take it."

"Ha! You're a genius," Shylock said to Balthasar and began sharpening a cruel-looking blade.

"I thought you were going to save my friend!" Bassanio said, scowling at Balthasar. "What've you done?"

Balthasar just winked at Bassanio, leaving him speechless. Why did the lawyer look so familiar?

Shylock took a step towards Antonio and raised the knife. "Looks like I win this one, Antonio!" he said.

"Wait!" Balthasar shouted, making the whole room jump. He looked at the contract again. "It says here, you're allowed to take a pound of flesh – "

"Yes, yes!" Shylock snapped.

"But no blood," Balthasar said, quietly.

Shylock froze. "What?"

"You can cut out your pound of Antonio's flesh, but it doesn't say you can spill any of his blood. Also, you can't take just over a pound, or just under a pound. It has to be exactly a pound of flesh. If it's more or less, you'll go to prison for murder!" Balthasar rolled up the paper again. "Go on then!"

Shylock trembled with rage and stared at Balthasar. Finally, he threw down his knife and stormed from the courtroom, defeated. The crowd cheered and Bassanio ran forwards and grabbed Balthasar's hand.

"How can we ever thank you, sir?" Bassanio said.

"Well, you can start by making sure that your friend doesn't make any more stupid deals," Balthasar said. The young man looked down at Bassanio's fingers. "I charge no fee but if you're truly grateful for your friend's life, you could give me that ring."

Bassanio pulled back as if he'd touched hot coals. "I'm sorry, sir, but I swore I'd never part with this ring."

The lawyer shrugged. "So ungrateful," he said. "You won't even give me a simple trinket to thank me for saving him."

Bassanio wanted to show how grateful he was, but he'd promised Portia that he'd guard the ring with his life. In the end, he pulled the ring from his finger and pressed it into Balthasar's hand. "Take it! Thank you for saving my friend's life!"

The lawyer hurried out of the room. Bassanio turned to Antonio. "I just hope Portia doesn't notice that the ring's gone!" he said.

6 The truth about the ring

Antonio and Bassanio hurried back to Portia's palace in Belmont, eager to tell her all about the adventure they'd had.

Portia was waiting them in the ballroom. Bassanio frowned; she seemed out of breath. "Are you all right, Portia?" he asked.

"Yes," she panted. "I just … ran … up some stairs … I was excited to … see you! Isn't … that right, Nerissa?"

"Quite right!" Nerissa agreed.

"So this is Antonio!" Portia said, changing the subject, quickly.

Antonio bowed low. "My lady, Bassanio told me you were beautiful, and now I'm glad I took such a risk to bring you two together," he said.

"So how did you free him?" Portia asked. "Did Shylock take the money?"

Bassanio laughed. "No," he said, handing back the bag of gold. "A very clever lawyer proved that Shylock's claim was wrong."

Portia frowned. "How could you afford a lawyer, Antonio?" She turned to Bassanio. "I hope you paid him well."

Bassanio could feel his face reddening, and slid his hand behind his back.

Portia noticed. "Where's the ring?" she said. "The one that I gave you?"

Bassanio fell to his knees. "Forgive me, Portia, I gave it to the lawyer. He insisted and I was so grateful to him."

"But you promised to keep it until you died!" Portia snapped. "How could you give away your wedding ring so easily?"

51

"It wasn't his fault, my lady," Antonio said, stepping forward. "Bassanio loves you with all his heart, I swear!"

"Well, it's a good job the ring isn't lost then," Portia said, lifting up her hand and wiggling her fingers.

Bassanio gasped – there was his ring! "But how?" he stammered. "Who, where – "

Portia laughed. "Poor Bassanio," she said. "You think you've got it all worked out. It was *me* who saved Antonio. From what you said, I knew Shylock wouldn't let Antonio off the deal. I knew you'd need a clever brain to outwit him. So as soon as you left, I disguised myself as the young lawyer, Balthasar, and followed you. So here's your ring *and don't lose it this time!*"

"So it was you all along!" Bassanio laughed. "I thought you looked familiar!"

Antonio bowed again. "Brains as well as beauty!" he declared. "Bassanio's a lucky man."

"He's a lucky man to have such a friend as you too, Antonio," Portia said, smiling. "He doesn't deserve either of us! Now, you missed the actual wedding but we haven't had the party. Coming?"

So Antonio linked arms with Portia, and Portia linked arms with Bassanio, and all three went into the great feasting hall for the biggest party Verona had ever seen.

Three caskets, three choices

greed

self-importance

54

loyalty

Ideas for reading

Written by Clare Dowdall, PhD
Lecturer and Primary Literacy Consultant

Reading objectives:
- check that the book makes sense to them, discussing their understanding and exploring the meaning of words in context
- draw inferences such as inferring characters' feelings, thoughts and motives from their actions, and justify inferences with evidence
- discuss and evaluate how authors use language, including figurative language, considering the impact on the reader
- provide reasoned justifications for their views

Spoken language objectives:
- articulate and justify answers, arguments and opinions
- participate in discussions, presentations, performances, role play, improvisations and debates

Curriculum links: PSHE – relationships

Resources: ICT for research; pens and paper

Build a context for reading

- Read the title and explain that *The Merchant of Venice* is a famous play by William Shakespeare.
- Check that children know what a merchant is, and discuss what a merchant does.
- Read the blurb to the children. Ask them to describe what a casket is, and to discuss how the three caskets might be different from one another (appearance, value, meaning).

Understand and apply reading strategies

- Turn to the cast list on pp2–3. Ask children to suggest why Portia/Balthasar are in the same portrait, and to identify the character shown on the front cover.
- Prepare a shared reading of Chapter 1. Allocate the characters to children, while you act as a narrator. Support expressive reading, and reread sections to develop fluency and voice.